The White Snake

WITHDRAWN

A TOON GRAPHIC BY

BEN NADLER

Based on a fairy tale by the Grimm Brothers

Editorial Director & Book Design: FRANÇOISE MOULY

Editor: PAUL KARASIK

Guest Editor: DASHIELL SPIEGELMAN

BEN NADLER'S artwork was drawn with India Ink on Bristol board and colored digitally.

FOR VISUAL READERS

TOON

GRAPHICS

A TOON Graphic™ © 2019 Ben Nadler & TOON Books, an imprint of RAW Junior, LLC, 27 Greene Street, New York, NY 10013. TOON Books® and TOON Graphics™ are trademarks of RAW Junior, LLC. All rights reserved. No part of this book may be used or reproduced in any manner whatsoever without written permission except in the case of brief quotations embodied in critical articles and reviews. Library of Congress Cataloging-in-Publication Data: Names: Nadler, Ben, adapter, artist. | Grimm, Jacob, 1785-1863. | Grimm, Wilhelm, 1786-1859. Title: The white snake : adapted from a fairy tale by the Grimm brothers / by Ben Nadler; with an afterword by Paul Karasik. Other titles: Weisse Schlange. English. Description: New York, NY : Toon Books, [2019] | Summary: A graphic novel adaptation of the tale of Randall, a young servant who eats a forbidden food, gains the ability to understand animals' speech, and attains great rewards. Identifiers: LCCN 2018040601 | Subjects: LCSH: Graphic novels. | CYAC: Graphic novels. | Human-animal communication--Fiction. | Household servants--Fiction. | Kings, queens, rulers, etc.--Fiction. | Fairy tales. Classification: LCC PZ7.7.N22 Whi 2019 | DDC 741.5/973--dc23 All our books are Smyth Sewn (the highest library-quality binding available) and printed with soy-based inks on acid-free, woodfree paper harvested from responsible sources. Printed in China by C&C Offset Printing Co., Ltd. Distributed to the trade by Consortium Book Sales & Distribution, a division of Ingram Content Group; orders (866) 400-5351; ips@ingramcontent.com; www.cbsd.com.

ISBN 978-1-943145-37-9 (hardcover)   ISBN 978-1-943145-38-6 (softcover)

19 20 21 22 23 24 C&C 10 9 8 7 6 5 4 3 2 1

W W W . T O O N - B O O K S . C O M

I wish I could be out there with them, roaming free.

Servant boy! WHERE are you? Come here now!

AND SO, RANDALL WALKED FOR DAYS AND DAYS...

I should have asked for a horse.

AT LAST! I thought I'd never make it!

HELP WANTED

HEY, this is my lucky day!

EVERY EVENING, RANDALL BROUGHT THE KING A SECRET FINAL DISH AT THE END OF HIS MEAL.

No peeking, Randall! I told you, nobody sees this but the king and me.

AND EVERY EVENING, RANDALL GREW MORE AND MORE CURIOUS.

Thank you, Randall. Now leave me.

MUNCH!
MUNCH!
MUNCH!

UNTIL FINALLY, ONE DAY, RANDALL COULD NO LONGER RESIST...

Nothing else in this castle is even the slightest bit mysterious...

The **SECRET** of Borisylvania **MUST** be beneath that cover!

GASP!

Goodbye, my friend!

ALONE AND HUNGRY, OUR HERO COMPLETES THE LONG AND ARDUOUS JOURNEY BACK TO KING ARNOLD'S CASTLE...

YOU? I remember you! You're the servant boy I sent to Borisylvania!

So— Did you learn King Boris's **SECRET**?

WELL??

May I speak with Princess Tilda instead?

Some time in a cell will loosen your tongue! **GUARDS!** Take him to the dungeon!

And so Randall was confined in an oubliette...

SIGH. Maybe I should have just told the king what he wanted to know.

He hasn't eaten his food for days.

Ask him if we can have it!

They've forgotten me. I'm going to spend the rest of my life here!

Psst! Randall!

Huh?

Princess, I wanted to tell you—

SSSH! I don't have a lot of time.

Just listen to me.

THE KING WAS AMAZED, BUT HE WOULD NOT YET MAKE GOOD ON HIS PROMISE.

You shall NOT marry my daughter until you have brought me the Golden Apple from the Tree of Life. It is said to bring wisdom.

It will be a long and arduous journey, but it will be your last. Return with the Golden Apple, and you WILL marry Princess Tilda.

No one knows where the Tree of Life grows. I'll NEVER find it!

I should have asked for a horse...

BUT AFTER MANY WEEKS...

It's no use!

I've found golden pears, grapes, and melons, but not a single sign of the Tree of Life.

I'll **NEVER** find the Golden Apple!

BONK!

OW!

THE YOUTH, FULL OF JOY, SET OUT HOMEWARD.

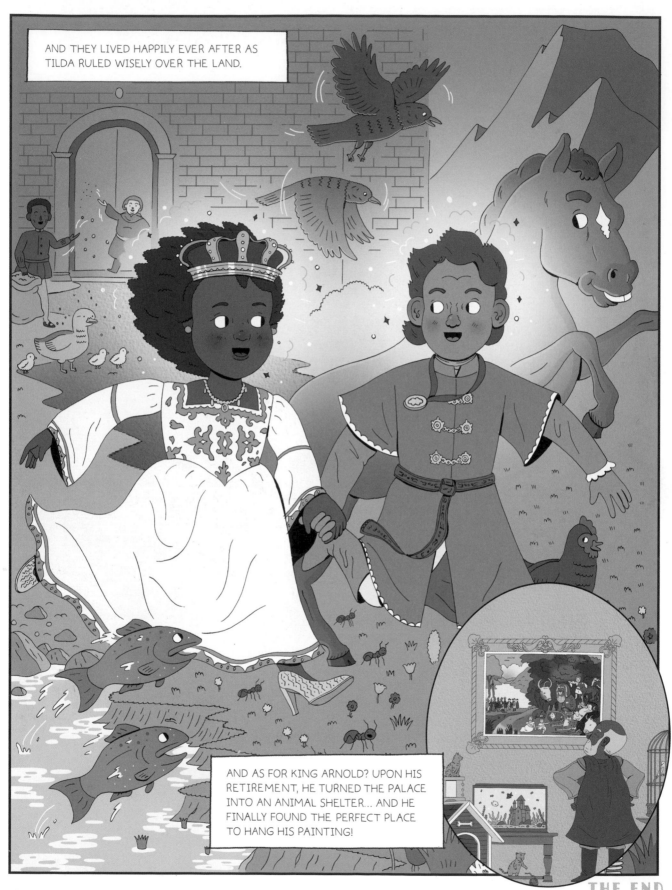

AND THEY LIVED HAPPILY EVER AFTER AS TILDA RULED WISELY OVER THE LAND.

AND AS FOR KING ARNOLD? UPON HIS RETIREMENT, HE TURNED THE PALACE INTO AN ANIMAL SHELTER... AND HE FINALLY FOUND THE PERFECT PLACE TO HANG HIS PAINTING!

THE END

56

FOLKTALES: TOLD AND RETOLD

by Paul Karasik

"The White Snake" appeared in the first edition of the German fairy and folk tales collected by Jacob and Wilhelm Grimm in 1812. The Brothers Grimm, educated at the University of Marburg, set out to preserve what they believed to be the genuine spirit of the German people by collecting the nation's folklore for future generations of scholars. Just as the Grimms' mission was to translate the stories from an oral tradition to a written tradition, cartoonist Ben Nadler has sought to tell the story in his medium, comics. This re-visioning is profoundly a part of the folktale tradition. Folktales are told and retold – and change. Over time, some aspects of a given tale stick, and others fall away. In the case of the Grimms, they culled their tales from storytellers, often women, who had themselves heard them from peasants. Folktales have no distinct authors but are the collective creation of generations of tellers, which makes them all the richer. As the novelist Italo Calvino said, quoting a Tuscan proverb, "The tale is not beautiful if nothing is added to it." And since they have no single author, there are no definitive versions of folktales. There are multiple versions – making it possible, in 1893, for Marian Roalfe Cox to compile three hundred and forty-five different tellings of "Cinderella." There are even varied tellings in the different editions of Grimm. After their initial success, the Grimms began to adapt the stories for an audience that included both scholars and children. All of this is to say that, although rightfully beloved, the Grimms' written versions are far from the "originals" – if such a thing could even exist.

WHAT IS DIFFERENT IN THIS MODERN RETELLING?

Just as many authors have retold and reconfigured the tales to suit their times and audiences, this volume is no exception. Depictions of gender roles, power, class, authority, and violence in the Grimms' tales reflect a different century. Our version of "The White Snake" continues that tradition of interpretation, adaptation, and re-visioning, including:

"Girl Power!": In the Grimms' version, the king's daughter is a shallow character. She's looking for a husband but cannot see the servant's virtues because of her proud heart. Our princess has the vision to see something special in Randall and the strength and intelligence to eventually inherit and rule the kingdom.

"A rose by any other name would smell as sweet:" "The servant" and "the king's daughter," nameless for the Grimms, were given the names Tilda

Clockwise from top left: Arthur Rackham illustration for a 1916 edition of the Grimms' tales; two of H. J. Ford's illustrations for the 1906 edition of *The Green Fairy Book*, edited by Andrew Lang; title page of the 1920 edition translated by Lucy Crane and "done into pictures" by her brother, Walter Crane.

and Randall by our cartoonist. Even the horse got a name: Edward.

"My kingdom for a horse!": Randall slays his horse to feed the fledgling ravens in the Grimms' telling, a memorable if gruesome detail. Here, the horse takes care of the raven babies until they learn to fly. The horse has also been given an engaging character, making the reader welcome him back when he reappears towards the conclusion.

"Long Live the Queen!": In the Grimms' story, the monarch of the ants is a king. We now know that ant colonies are, in fact, organized around their queens.

"Peace be with you!": Our version ends with the revelation that the painting that the king has been fretting over during the story is *The Peaceable Kingdom*, by Edward Hicks, a 19th-century American artist. Hicks was so devoted to the idea of all creatures living in harmony that he painted sixty-two versions of that scene.

"What's the big idea?!": Fairy tales are rarely interested in the motives behind the characters' thoughts or actions. The new first act, before the revelation of the contents of the dish, encourages readers to care. By the time the snake dinner is introduced, the reader already sympathizes with Randall and hopes for his success.

WHAT IS THE SAME IN THIS MODERN RETELLING?

The core of a folktale endures through its many retellings. At the center of this tale are the talking animals. Over the centuries, and in tales from around the world, there are many animal helpers or tricksters, such as Coyote in Native American folklore, Anansi the spider from Africa, Brer Rabbit from the African American traditions, and the European Puss In Boots. A Chinese folktale called "The Legend of the White Snake" tells of an immortal white snake spirit able to turn into a woman.

Often, snakes in folktales behave like ... snakes, treacherous and evil. In Aesop's "The Farmer and the Viper," for example, a farmer rescues a frozen snake which then attacks him, giving rise to the idiom "to nourish a viper in one's bosom" (not a good idea!). Just as treacherous is the snake in the Bible, who gives Eve some very bad advice about an apple from a special tree. Though it also features a couple, a snake, and an apple from an exalted tree, "The White Snake" tells a different story. (This animal role reversal would have been obvious to the Grimms' original audience: the Bible is the all-time best-selling book in Germany — and the second is Grimms'.)

The ancestor of a tale in which an encounter with a snake leads to wisdom – not death – might be in Greek mythology. In the tale of Melampus, a soothsayer gets his power by helping snakes and in return is given the ability to heal. Similarly, the king in "The Language of Animals," one of the ancient Jātaka tales from India, or the shepherd in "A Snake's Gift," a Serbian tale, acquire their ability to understand the speech of animals, "even ants," after

Top to bottom: The Peaceable Kingdom, by Edward Hicks, 1826, in the National Gallery of Art, Washington, D.C.; A printed card of Saint Francis talking to birds and animals; Orpheus Charming the Animals, by Jacob Hoefnagel, 1613, in the Morgan Library & Museum in New York City.